ROSIE'S WALK

Pat Hutchins

Rosie's Walk

RED FOX

Books by Pat Hutchins:

The Shrinking Mouse
Ten Red Apples
Don't Forget the Bacon
We're Going on a Picnic

ROSIE'S WALK
A RED FOX BOOK 978 0 099 41399 8

First published in Great Britain by The Bodley Head,
an imprint of Random House Children's Books

The Bodley Head edition published 1968
Red Fox edition published 2001

13 15 17 19 20 18 16 14 12

Copyright © Pat Hutchins, 1968
Copyright renewed © Pat Hutchins, 1996

Red Fox Books are published by Random House Children's Books,
61–63 Uxbridge Road, London W5 5SA.
Addresses for companies within The
Random House Group Limited can be
found at:
www.randomhouse.co.uk/offices.htm

A CIP catalogue record for this book is available from the British Library.

Printed in Singapore

*For Wendy
and Stephen*

Rosie the hen went for a walk

across the yard

around
the
pond

over the haycock

past the mill

through the fence

under the beehives

and
got back
in time
for dinner.